Anonymous

Babouscka

A Russian Christmas Story and Other Stories

Anonymous

Babouscka
A Russian Christmas Story and Other Stories

ISBN/EAN: 9783743390614

Manufactured in Europe, USA, Canada, Australia, Japa

Cover: Foto ©Andreas Hilbeck / pixelio.de

Manufactured and distributed by brebook publishing software
(www.brebook.com)

Anonymous

Babouscka

BABOUSCKA
A RUSSIAN
CHRISTMAS STORY

AND
OTHER
STORIES

Illustrated

The Werner Company

NEW YORK   AKRON, OHIO   CHICAGO

1899

THE LAST TRIP.

BABOUSCKA.

OUT OF BREATH, TIRED, YET HUR-
RYING ON.

IF you were a Russian child you would not watch to see Santa Klaus come down the chimney; but you would stand by the windows to catch a peep at poor Babouscka as she hurries by.

Who is Babouscka? Is she Santa Klaus' wife?

No, indeed. She is only a poor little crooked wrinkled old woman, who comes at Christmas time into everybody's house, who peeps into every cradle, turns back every coverlid, drops a tear on the baby's white pillow, and goes away very, very sorrowful.

And not only at Christmas time, but through all the cold winter, and especially in March, when the wind blows loud, and whistles and howls and dies away like a sigh, the Russian children hear the rustling step of the Babouscka. She is always in a hurry. One hears her running fast along the crowded streets and over the quiet country fields. She seems to be out of breath and tired, yet she hurries on.

Whom is she trying to overtake?

She scarcely looks at the little children as they press their rosy faces against the window pane and whisper to each other, " Is the Babouscka looking for us ? "

No, she will not stop ; only on Christmas eve will she come up-stairs into the nursery and give each little one a present. You must not think she leaves handsome gifts such as Santa Klaus brings for you. She does not bring bicycles to the boys or French dolls to the girls. She does not come in a gay little sleigh drawn by reindeer, but hobbling along on foot, and she leans on a crutch. She has her old apron filled with candy and cheap toys, and the children all love her dearly. They watch to see her come, and when one hears a rustling, he cries, "Lo! the Babouscka!" then all others look, but one must turn one's head very quickly or she vanishes. I never saw her myself.

Best of all, she loves little babies, and often, when the tired mothers sleep, she bends over their cradles, puts her brown, wrinkled face close down to the pillow and looks very sharply.

What is she looking for?

Ah, that you can't guess unless you know her sad story.

Long, long ago, a great many yesterdays ago, the Babouscka, who was even then an old woman, was busy sweeping her little hut. She lived in the coldest corner of cold Russia, and she lived alone in a lonely place where four wide roads met. These roads were at this time white with snow, for it was winter time. In the summer, when the fields were full of flowers and the air full of sunshine and singing birds, Babouscka's home did not seem so very quiet; but in the winter, with only the snow-flakes and the shy snow-birds and the loud wind for company, the little old woman felt very cheerless. But she was a busy old woman, and as it was already twilight, and her home but half swept, she felt in a great hurry to finish her work before bed-time. You must know the Babouscka was poor and could not afford to do her work by candle-light.

Presently, down the widest and the lonesomest of the white roads, there appeared a long train of people coming. They were walking slowly, and seemed to be asking each other questions as to which way they should take. As the procession came nearer, and finally stopped outside the little hut, Babouscka was frightened at the splendor. There were Three Kings, with crowns on their heads, and the jewels on the Kings' breastplates sparkled like sunlight. Their heavy fur cloaks were white with the falling snow-flakes, and the queer humpy camels on which they rode looked white as milk in the snow-storm. The harness on the camels was decorated with gold, and plates of silver adorned the saddles. The saddle-cloths were of the richest Eastern stuffs, and all the servants had the dark eyes and hair of an Eastern people.

The slaves carried heavy loads on their backs, and each of the Three Kings carried a present. One carried a beautiful transparent jar, and in the fading light Babouscka could see in it a golden liquid which she knew from its color must be myrrh. Another had in his hand a richly woven bag, and it seemed to be heavy, as indeed it was, for it was full of gold. The third had a stone vase in his hand, and from the rich perfume which filled the snowy air, one could guess the vase to have been filled with incense.

Babouscka was terribly frightened, so she hid herself in her hut, and let the servants knock a long time at her door before she dared open it and answer their questions as to the road they should take to a far-away town. You know she had never studied a geography lesson in her life, was old and stupid and scared. She knew the way across the fields to the nearest village, but she knew nothing else of all the wide world full of cities. The servants scolded, but the Three Kings spoke kindly to her, and asked her to accompany them on their journey that she might show them the way as far as she knew it. They told her, in words so simple that she could camels' feet were covered by the deep white snow. Everything was the same as usual ; and to make sure that the night's visitors had not been a fancy, she found her old broom hanging on a peg behind the door, where she had put it when the servants knocked.

Now that the sun was shining, and she remembered the glitter of the gold and the smell of the sweet gums and myrrh, she wished she had gone with the travellers.

And she thought a great deal about the little Baby the Three Kings had gone to worship. She had no children of her own — nobody loved her — ah, if she had only gone! The more she brooded on the thought, the more miserable she grew, till the very sight of her home became hateful to her.

It is a dreadful feeling to realize that one has lost a chance of happiness. There is a feeling called remorse that can gnaw like a sharp little tooth. Babouscka felt this little tooth cut into her heart every time she remembered the visit of the Three Kings.

After a while the thought of the Little Child

not fail to understand, that they had seen a Star in the sky and were following it to a little town where a young Child lay. The snow was in the sky now, and the Star was lost out of sight.

"Who is the Child?" asked the old woman.

"He is a King, and we go to worship him," they answered. "These presents of gold, frankincense and myrrh are for Him. When we find Him we will take the crowns off our heads and lay them at His feet. Come with us, Babouscka!"

What do you suppose? Shouldn't you have thought the poor little woman would have been glad to leave her desolate home on the plains to accompany these Kings on their journey?

But the foolish woman shook her head. No, the night was dark and cheerless, and her little home was warm and cosy. She looked up into the sky, and the Star was nowhere to be seen. Besides, she wanted to put her hut in order — perhaps she would be ready to go to-morrow. But the Three Kings could not wait; so when to-morrow's sun rose they were far ahead on their journey. It seemed like a dream to poor Babouscka, for even the tracks of the became her first thought at waking and her last at night. One day she shut the door of her house forever, and set out on a long journey. She had no hope of overtaking the Three Kings, but she longed to find the Child, that she too might love and worship Him. She asked every one she met, and some people thought her crazy, but others gave her kind answers. Have you perhaps guessed that the young Child whom the Three Kings sought was our Lord himself?

People told Babouscka how He was born in a manger, and many other things which you children have learned long ago. These answers puzzled the old dame mightily. She had but one idea in her ignorant head. The Three Kings had gone to seek a Baby. She would, if not too late, seek Him too.

She forgot, I am sure, how many long years had gone by. She looked in vain for the Christ-child in His manger-cradle. She spent all her little savings in toys and candy so as to make friends with little children, that they might not run away when she came hobbling into their nurseries.

Now you know for whom she is sadly seeking

when she pushes back the bed-curtains and bends down over each baby's pillow. Sometimes, when the old grandmother sits nodding by the fire, and the bigger children sleep in their beds, old Babouscka comes hobbling into the room, and whispers softly, " Is the young Child here?"

Ah, no; she has come too late, too late. But the little children know her and love her. Two thousand years ago she lost the chance of finding Him. Crooked, wrinkled, old, sick and sorry, she yet lives on, looking into each baby's face — always disappointed, always seeking. Will she find Him at last?

A FOREIGN EMBASSY.

NESTLED in a secluded nook between two ranges of billowy hills, with one dormer window commanding a bend of the Hudson, but with its ample porch facing the gorge which led like a steep staircase to the wilderness, stood for many years the hunting lodge of Peter Van Vechten.

It had a wild, solitary look, and yet there were signs of comfort and even of luxury about the place. Its lonely situation might have been the choice of either a very happy or of a grief-stricken man. At all events it was the hermitage of a man who loved to live apart from the world. The broad carriage-drive which swept up to the hospitable porch was grass-grown and had lost all signs of ruts of wheels. Only hoof-prints here and there told that Peter Van Vechten was as fond of the hunt as ever, and that his daughter Lilian often rode to the hounds with him.

He had been a kind and true father to his little girl, almost too indulgent for her own best good, parting with her company much of the time that she might acquire an elegant education in the city, and living a lonely life with only his three hounds as companions. At length Lilian's education was pronounced finished, and she returned to the Lodge. The little window that kept watch over the Hudson was her own, and she would look at the passengers flitting by in the swift-winged schooners on their way to Albany or New York, for this was before the time of steamboats or rail-car. It was very dull at the Lodge, in spite of rides upon her pony, and the harpsichord which her father loved to listen to in the evening. He had a rich full voice and sometimes joined her in

" My heart's in the highlands."

He escorted her in her calls at the stately old manor-houses, and once in a great while a venerable coach rattled up to their own door and a Madam Livingston or Van Cortland, or a Miss Verplanck would make a dignified visit at the Lodge.

There were the woods for botanizing and her embroidery frame for rainy days, but in spite of all this, Lilian was discontented. She could not have cared greatly for her father, and yet she was jealous of his pets, the three great dogs with their odd names: Prince, Peace and Prosper; so-called, their master explained, because if you held fast to Principle, Peace and Prosperity would follow. Prince was in fact the leader of the little pack, and if you held him well in leash, the others never wandered. Peace was a quiet inoffensive dog, a poor hunter, with a loving disposition and a melting eye. Old Prosper was always lucky, and would come leaping back with the game lightly, but securely held in his deep jaws, while Prince looked on with the air of a commanding general.

Lilian wondered that her father could be so happy in the society of these dumb friends. His easy-going temper grated against her ambitious spirit. She chafed at the Lodge, not so much because she was lonely and longed for pleasant companionship, for friends to love, for opportunities to do good, as that her proud, imperious nature longed for continual admiration. She did not care whether anyone really loved her, provided she could be envied, praised and flattered.

When winter began she moped and sulked, and fancied herself the most unhappy girl in the world, until early in December an invitation came from an aunt in Philadelphia, urging her to spend two months in that city. Philadelphia was then the seat of government, and a gay and fashionable centre. Lilian was delighted. She did not ask herself whether her father might not be lonely in her absence, nor did she for a moment suspect that he had written her aunt requesting this invitation — she was simply overjoyed to leave the Lodge and to think that new dresses and invitations to routs and parties awaited her.

But even in Philadelphia Lilian was not quite happy. The society in which she was thrown was political, and young ladies were honored quite as much from their fathers' positions as for their own grace or beauty. It was mortifying to Lilian to see

Miss Van Rensselaer of Albany leading the contra dance, just because, as she told her jealous heart, Miss Van Rensselaer's papa was a great man. How provoking, too, to count Edith Verplanck's bouquets and the admirers hovering round Gertrude Van Cortland's chair! She was sure Cora Livingston's entrance would not have caused such a sensation if her father had not recently been appointed Minister to France. No one had heard of Peter Van Vechten, and she asked herself with tears in her eyes why her father had not done something to render himself famous and confer distinction upon his family.

Her two months stretched into four, but she returned to the Lodge more discontented than ever. Her father greeted her gladly. He had employed himself in her absence in making alterations in the house which he thought would please her fancy; and he proposed to invite Gertrude Van Cortland to pass the summer with her. Lilian declined the offer ungraciously, and met all her father's efforts for her pleasure with an ungrateful manner which refused to be pleased with anything. Her father was very considerate and gentle in these days; he did not reprove

"GONE AWAY."

or reproach her, but seemed to be silently trying to find the way to his daughter's heart. There was a tender yearning in the furtive way in w.iich he watched her, a glad flushing of the cheek whenever she chanced to bestow on him a careless caress. He was not well and had given up hunting; but he went into society more than formerly, and Lilian could not help noticing when she entered a drawing-room leaning upon his arm, that there was a little lull in conversation and people looked at him admiringly. He was a handsome man with his abundant gray hair and fine soldierly figure — she contrasted him thankfully with stout little Mr. Van Rensselaer, and felt that she would be proud of him even in a Philadelphia assemblage of diplomats and dignitaries. If only she could hear his name called with some high-sounding title attached! Perhaps it was not too late even now. "Father," she asked one day as they rode through the wood together, "why don't you go into politics?"

He leaned forward and gently caressed the head of one of the hounds with the handle of his riding-whip. "If I went into politics, Lilian," he replied, "I would have to leave the Lodge and perhaps bid farewell to Principle, Peace and Prosperity."

Lilian thought of the words only as the names of the dogs. " I don't see why you are so attached to them," she replied, " I was so ashamed all last winter to have people say when I was introduced, 'Van Vechten, it seems to me I knew your father — let me see — wasn't he a member of Congress for —— ' or 'are you the daughter of Colonel or of Judge Van Vechten.' Then some of the Philadelphia families are descended from earls and dukes, and have coats of arms emblazoned on the panels of their coaches. I never could find that any of *our* family were noble : — and one or two of the girls have been to England and have been presented at court. Edith Verplanck showed me an amber satin dress she wore at a royal reception, to which she was invited just because her father had been sent on a diplomatic mission. *I* don't seem to have *anything* to be proud of ! "

Lilian's father glanced aside. " I am sorry you have had occasion to be ashamed of your father," he said quietly.

The girl's better nature asserted itself for the

moment. "I never could be ashamed of you, dear, kind father," she cried impulsively. "It is just because you are so much more worthy than other men that I fret that you are not recognized. I should think our country would feel honored to be able to point to you as its minister in some European city. I am every bit as proud of you as Cora Livingston is of her father — she always looked so aggravatingly happy when people praised him to her."

"But Lilian, if I were to be sent upon a foreign mission, perhaps I could not take you with me. How would you like being left behind?"

"I should not mind it in the least," Lilian exclaimed thoughtlessly. "I should hear people praising you, and so would Cora and Gertrude and the other girls; and I could hold up my head with any of them."

"And you would not mind if I were to spend the rest of my days in Turkey or India?"

"You would not have to spend your whole life there, would you?" Lilian asked; "if you did, couldn't you find some way for me to join you?"

"And leave Philadelphia? are you sure that you would care to?"

"Why of course, dear father."

"Even if it were a half civilized post, something like the Lodge?"

"Yes indeed; and to prove it I'll not leave you this winter. I am afraid I have been a selfish daughter, and I will give up Philadelphia if you wish it."

A smile of infinite content crossed Peter Van Vechten's face, but he shook his head. "No, no, the sacrifice would be too great — you enjoy Philadelphia even though you are not a grandee's daughter, and you shall go again this winter."

Lilian had forgotten this conversation, when just before leaving for her second winter with her aunt, as the stage was climbing the hill and the servant carrying out her little cow-skin covered trunk and well corded cedarn boxes, her father took her hand and spoke hurriedly as though moved by sudden impulse : "And Lilian one last word: if I should obtain a foreign mission and go away — I know you love me child, but don't grieve — I'll manage some way to send for you, so be glad of my promotion."

Lilian was delighted; was it possible that her

father was keeping back a secret as a glad surprise for her some day ! She kissed him rapturously, sprang into the coach, and waving a pretty silk-mittened hand to the lonely man standing there with the dogs capering about him and striving in vain to console him, she rolled gaily away toward Philadelphia.

Very touching and tender were the letters which came to Lilian in the early winter, they were brief however, and infrequent, and sometimes, in a pause in the gay whirl of excitement in which she found herself, Lilian would wonder why her father wrote so seldom. Perhaps he was busy with negotiations in regard to the foreign ministry or embassy. He referred to it sometimes in a sentence like this :

" Don't be ashamed of your old father ; a prospect of high honor opens before him; " or " When I am gone don't forsake Principle, and may Peace and Prosperity never desert you."

Occasionally he spoke of a "long journey ; " but though Lilian wrote enthusiastically, or curiously, and begged him to confide his projects to her, he kept his secret well.

One dismal day in February Lilian was quite alone.

Her aunt was slightly ill and kept her room. A fine sleety rain drove against the windows, and the room was damp and chill. She seated herself at the harpsichord and played the old melodies which her father loved to hear. She was singing:

> "My heart's in the highlands,
> My heart is not here,"

when a servant handed her a letter. It was from her father, but in such a cramped and trembling hand that she hardly recognized it.

"DEAREST LILIAN, (it ran)

The message has come at last. I have received my commission, and must leave soon for a far country. I have dreaded the passage, but now I am contented. I long only to see you before I go. I fear that you may be unhappy without me; but be comforted — we shall not be long separated. '*I go to prepare a place for you that where I am there you may be also.*' Come quickly to bid me good-bye, for I may be summoned at any moment. It is a great honor, and I am very happy. Take care of Principle for me, and may Peace and Prosper be yours, always.　　　　　Your loving

FATHER."

When Lilian's aunt read the letter she looked pale

and frightened. "You must go at once, poor child," she said.

"Of course," Lilian replied, and hurriedly prepared for her journey. How odd, she thought, that her father had not mentioned the name of the foreign country to which he was sent. No matter, it was enough to know that the embassy was an honorable and an important one. She had always been proud of her father; she was not surprised that he should be chosen for such a mission; and now her delighted imagination pictured the homage which she would receive as the daughter of a foreign minister. Her father need not have feared that she would miss him — she had grown accustomed to their separation and it did not pain her. He had said that she should come too. She hoped the station would prove gay and interesting, one of the principal capitals of Europe, and she almost regretted her rash expression of willingness to follow her father to some remote exile.

The stage left her at the wayside tavern a half a mile from the Lodge. She was surprised not to find her father here to meet her, and questioned the innkeeper, who seemed embarrassed at meeting her.

"Your father has gone away, Miss," he stammered.

"Is it possible?" Lilian cried; "am I too late? He must have been sent for suddenly."

"Yes Miss, he was took very sudden, at the last," replied the man.

There was nothing to do but to climb the hill, vexed that she had had her journey for nothing, and wondering what messages her father might have left for her with the housekeeper.

As she opened the gate, Peace laid his great muzzle affectionately against her hand, and Prince leaped joyfully; but old Prosper only looked toward the house and howled. So preoccupied was she with her own thoughts that it was not until she stood upon the very threshold that she noticed a long scarf of crape which fluttered from the knocker.

Then all the awful force of the words, "Gone away," struck the girl. Her grief was intensified by her remorse for her selfish behavior, and for a time she wept for her father as one who could not be comforted. He had been very ill, so the housekeeper told her, all winter; but he would not allow any one to alarm Lilian. He wrote to her from time to time

8

when quite unable to do so. He spoke of her lovingly but refused to have her sent for.

He had said once, after reading one of her eager questioning letters asking where he was going, " Tell her this is the guide-book. She will find the city all described here."

Lilian took up the worn Bible and found a mark at the passage :

"*Eye hath not seen, nor ear heard, neither hath it entered into the heart of man, the things which God hath prepared for them that love Him.*"

Then she remembered that her father had said that she should join him some day, and she knew how little she deserved such an honor as this. She lacked the graces suited to the daughter of an ambassador to the Heavenly City. She remembered that Cora Livingston had said, "I have to be very careful of my conduct — my father's position demands it;" and that Edith Verplanck had told her that she was more frightened than glad when she knew that she was to be presented at court, for she feared that she might make some mistake in etiquette in the presence of the king.

"The King of that world" — thought Lilian; and she sat herself earnestly to a study of the code of sweet and gentle courtesy which made Christ "the most perfect gentleman of all time ;" and to the acquirement of accomplishments which she might carry with her sometime when she joined the celestial embassy. Little by little the spirit of Christ grew within her, she became more meek and loving and trusting, and serving her king, she became widely known among the poor and suffering as the "kindly lady."

An embroidered satin picture, of the kind that were fashionable when our grandmothers were young, hangs still over the little mantle of the chamber overlooking the Hudson, and on a species of memorial tablet which adorns its centre, is delicately worked in faded silk this stanza :

> " My boast is not that I deduced my birth
>   From kings enthroned, and rulers of the earth ;
> But higher far my proud pretentions rise,
>   The child of parents passed into the skies."

I talked in this room with a bent old woman, who, in her girlhood days had been the dressing maid of aged Mistress Van Vechten. "Her senses failed her at the last," said the old tiring-woman, "for she took a strange notion that she was the daughter of a foreign embassador. She grew restless like— and used to say that she wanted to go to 'the embassy.' She had always been so simple-minded and unostentatious that it seemed all the queerer to see her taking such a high fancy. The very dumb animals loved her. I've heard her repeat the names of a pack of hounds that used to belong to her father. 'Peace and Prosper,' she'd say; 'keep Principle and you'll always have Peace and Prosper.' She was a dear, kind lady. The night before she left us, she came out of her room. 'Get my best brocade, Calisty,' says she, 'I am going to the embassy. My white brocade with the gold-thread figure—I must look my best—in the presence of the king.' Then she let me put her to bed as peaceable as a child; but about midnight she sat up. 'It's my turn, Calisty,' she cried, her voice all trembling with happiness, 'it's my turn,—didn't you hear the usher call Ambassador Van Vechten's daughter?'"

"I lighted a candle as quick as I could; the dear soul was gone."

A QUEER LETTER CARRIER.

MOST children have seen a United States post-man, with his plain uniform and letter-bag. The letter carrier's quick step, too, you have noticed, as if he were walking for a prize.

Now I will tell you of a postman who wore no uniform, never uttered a word to any one he met, and always distributed his mail without being late. He could not read a word, and yet gave the mail to the right person. He had no salary, got up and went to bed when he pleased, and though he had not a dollar in the world, he was contented. The queerest thing about him is that I can't tell you his name, nor did he wear a number, as some carriers do. Moreover, he carried letters in the country and not in the city ; and this, too, one hundred and fifty years ago. Through the woods he walked on his round, and if it came to be dark, there were no lights to guide him. When he got to the place where he delivered the letters, he did not pull the bell with a quick jerk, as the postman does, nor knock, to summon some one to come and get the mail. If any one thanked him for the mail he brought, he never said, " You're welcome." Altogether, as you must admit, he was a funny letter-man.

But the funniest thing is that he was not a letter-man at all. He was a letter-dog. More than one hundred and fifty years ago, by the aid of the General Court of Massachusetts, there was built by the settlers of Brunswick and Topsham (on the Androscoggin River, in the district of Maine) a fort named Fort George, as a defence against the Indians. A picture of these ancient works shows that it was made of stone, with little windows, like port-holes, near the top of the walls. Within was a house, and the roof peers over the ramparts. A flag floats from the staff, and a heavy door is in the front — a point carefully guarded. Barracks for fifteen men were provided — a small force, but enough to keep the Indians at a distance.

About ten miles away, on the Kennebec River, was

a little settlement called "The Reach," where now the city of Bath, a famous ship-building place, is pleasantly built along the river bank. The very few families living at "The Reach" kept up communication with the fort, for it was their place of refuge in war, and supplies were to be bought there in quiet times.

The mail route of the carrier I am telling you about was from this fort to "The Reach," through places where Indians were hidden, waiting for some white man to come within reach of their arrows. The faithful dog would carry packages of letters from Brunswick to the settlement, and bring back answers. When he got to the house at "The Reach," where the mail was to stop, he would howl in an anxious way; then the letters would be taken from him; but still he would wait and not stir until another bundle was given him — the parcel of mail matter for those in the fort. Then he would put the letters, not in a letter-bag, but in a place more safe — his mouth!

Off he would start again through the lonely forest. Foxes and rabbits and birds might start up near him, but he remembered his errand, and turned neither to the right nor to the left. In two hours he would cover the distance, and howl at the fort gate for the mail to be taken in. In case of great danger, when word would be written, the dog would always rush away as if he knew what was the matter!

I wish I could tell you that, after working hard and faithfully, the wise dog died quietly at home; but, alas! after a while the Indians discovered that the dog oft seen was conveying information from the fort to the houses down the river, and they soon found a chance to kill him. At last, one day when he was trotting through the thicket, holding fast to his parcel, a slight sound was heard, which his instinct told him was the light tread of a fox; but the next instant an Indian burst through the underbrush, and death overtook him then and there! A brave man dies, and praise is given him long after: the trusty dog falls when he is doing his duty, and not even his name is recorded!

THE QUAKER WEDDING.

DURING the wars with England, the inhabitants of Nantucket, notwithstanding their hardships and privations, persisted in marriages and weddings. Father Peleg, though he had seen two ships full-laden with sperm oil, belonging to "himself and sons," taken by the enemy just off Great Point, never thought of postponing William's marriage. The time for its solemnization was appointed for the "twelfth day of the twelfth month" by the monthly meeting. That which was dictated to this "body of Friends" by the "moving of the spirit," silenced all argument. Accordingly the nuptials of Peleg's son and Andrew's daughter were duly to be recognized.

THE MEETING HOUSES

used by Friends were devoid of paint, as a matter of

discipline. The interior was divided by a line of pillars, separating the half occupied by the men from what was denominated the "women's part." These posts were longitudinally grooved. At times of business, there descended straight from the heavens, the children believed, between every two pillars a sliding door, giving each sex a chance for private discussions.

At their public gatherings, these doors were again raised, every boy and girl quietly wondering how! There were no Signor Blitzes in those parts; tables had always quietly rested on four legs, unless a caster was off, which was soon remedied.

At right angles with the posts, and gradually elevated from a square in the centre of each apartment and terminated by the wall, were two opposing sets of "rising-seats." If the simile is admissible (if not, let it pass) the arrangement is as that of a circus, ignoring the literal meaning of the word, and considering it an "oblong square." The last sentence, although written, understood and countenanced by a birth-right member, is, it must be confessed, objectionable as a matter of taste. The *figure* holds its own.

The "rising-seats" fronting the congregation were occupied by ministers, elders and overseers. On the ground benches sat "members of meeting" generally. On the back "rising-seats," facing the ministers, etc., sat the gay people—men who wore double-breasted coats; girls with bows on their bonnets; women who insisted upon carrying a closed parasol by the rightful handle, instead of the apex; and those who had yet other worldly ways.

On an occasion of a "marriage-in-meeting," one of the overseers' "rising-seats " in the women's division was left vacant for the "bridal couple," two old men who were to superintend the groom, and two old women who had the care of the bride.

According to appointment, one cold week-day morning, William and Lydia walked, arm in arm, through a crowded assembly, to the second rising-seat in the Friends' South Meeting-house. As soon as seated, the two old men alluded to took their places by William, and the two old women by Lydia.

The twelve eyes were riveted on the floor. "At what are they gazing?" thought the young folks.

Little Jedidah Hussey solved the question to her

own satisfaction: "they were all watching a winter fly, which they feared might come to life and disturb one of the folds in Lydia's shawl, and it would be *such* a shame!"

Jedidah must be excused, for she belonged to a Presbyterian family. She had never been to a Quaker meeting before, or she would have known that the eight eyes were intent on the "inner light," while the other four were cast down by the weight of the impending silence, their owners respectively trying to recite their *rôle*.

THE SIGNAL.

It is incumbent upon the Friend who sits next to the young man, when in his judgment the minute has arrived for the ceremony to begin, to signify the same to the groom. This is brought about by a slight touch of the arm. William, being on the lookout for this, as the time draws near clears his throat repeatedly; looks up inquiringly and defiantly, almost with a nod, at the junction of the ceiling with the wall at the farthest end of the room, as if calculating some patent improvement. Suddenly he is interested in the nails of the floor. He counts them: first down; then up; then across; half diagonally; and whole ditto. Finally, to verify his mathematics and to prove his entire calmness, he ascertains the number of rows and the units in each row, and is about to get the product, when the dreaded sign is given.

He has half a mind to rub his crazy-bone, as though the nudge has fallen on a tender spot, thereby showing the audience his stoicism. Instead of which the color leaves his lips as he attempts to get up. He reaches for the right hand of the bride, to aid the weaker vessel to find her feet.

Lydia, on the other side, persists in extending the left; knows confidently that the "left *was* the right" when they practised the night before, and the week before, and the month before. The stronger sex gains, at last; with right hands joined they rise and face the — (Query: What?)

They pause a moment; Jedidah thinks, "in order to give the girls a chance to see what the bride was dressed in."

As to that, the groom's attire would bear scrutiny. Thus: wash-leather short-clothes, silver knee-buckles, rose-colored silk stockings reaching to the knees, black swallow-tail coat, white vest (material — lost to tradition) and, to crown the whole, a "broad brim" which was studiously kept on the head during the whole meeting.

Bride's: Pearl-colored silk skirt and wrapper — the former open in front disclosing an apron of the same fabric, just one shade deeper; on her head the primmest of prim "*pleater*" (no! *plaiter* is *not* the right! what do modern spelling-matches know of bonnets worn by original Friends!) — and over her shoulders was thrown (thrown! indeed! rather put on with line and plummet and level and a little mariner's compass!) a book-muslin kerchief.

THE CEREMONY.

In this garb they address the meeting. He speaks first — that is, he shall speak when he gets ready; always did have his own way, and guesses he shan't alter just now; has some idea of saying, in a jocose

way to the congregation, that he shall "bide his
time;" wishes he hadn't sat in that draft and got cold
in his limbs, which makes his knees shake, though
nothing new. At length, throat effectually cleared,
he declares in a voice of thunder that he takes Lydia
to be his wife. His tones come out on the last two
or three words with a bound so loud that it is evident,
he thinks, to the audience, how self-possessed he is.

The bride then repeats the same, telling them in a
"confidential whisper" that she takes William to be
her husband.

The latter is quite relieved when Lydia gets to the
period; his only fear had been for days, that *she*
would break down. He winks at her to that effect
as they resume their seats. She looks no response,
though she *did* know that the voice in which her
husband went through his part was one totally new
and strange to her. (This secret she kept inviolate
till the twenty-fifth anniversary of their wedding-day.)

As the couple sat down, the strangers rose to de-
part, when the rustling of paper brought them into
quiet again. A certificate of great dimensions was
handed to the couple for them to sign in their new

relation, setting forth what had taken place. When William took the parchment he examined it thoroughly, determined to know to what he was about to put his name. No one of the congregation suspected that he had hired Seth Gardner to copy this document (Seth wrote German text like a native), and that he and Lydia had viewed it again and again ; had even tried holding a pen over the "places elect" of their names, that nothing should be imperfectly done on the day of the marriage. But, alas ! they had never spoken in meeting before, and the rehearsing went for very little. They signed ; he his old name, she her new.

There were those who said " if Lydia had removed her right kid, which extended to the elbow, the play of the fore-arm and the freedom of the thimble-finger would have given an ease to her handwriting which was entirely omitted." But there always *are* fault-finders !

After the above signatures were obtained, the certificate was read to the meeting at large by the clerk of the men's part, who took his stand on the women's side of the posts. The autograph of the crowd was then allowed.

A silence ensued, less anxious than that which preceded the ceremony; a "refreshing season"! One aged man felt moved to give the newly married couple his sympathy.

A few more moments of intense hush, when the head of each department, simultaneously inspired to shake hands each with the other, performed this feat across the dividing pilaster, as a signal that "meeting was out."

THE FEAST.

No more interesting sight can be found than that of a long table spread in a Quaker's side-room, surrounded by youth and maidens in the simple dress of the sect. That day two tables were arranged for the guests. The bride and groom, both under twenty-one years of age, yet being married, must sit with the elder and more staid persons. At their table, the drab coat prevailed, the muslin cap neatly pinned beneath the chin, and the silk mit. The old men's neckerchiefs seemed to preserve an unparalleled parallelism. The end of Jacob's tie protruded a half-inch from the knot. The end of Benjamin's tie protruded a half-inch from the knot. The same of Laban's, the same of every other. Each man spread a large red bandanna over his knees; every woman a substantial Irish-linen pocket handkerchief in her lap. A beautiful picture! The table itself was appointed with the real "dark blue" direct from Canton, heavy silver, and cut-glass from the old country; no plated ware! no burglars!

The other table was surrounded by the young of both sexes — the boys with hair uniformly cut in "bowl-fashion;" nothing more nor less than the "bang" of to-day, if spoken aside. The faces of the girls peeped out of the sheerest round-eared caps that you ever saw; the white of the muslin only adding to the innocence of the visage, and bringing out, in a stronger light, the lurking fun of sweet sixteen.

Before "Friends" commenced eating, a long and painful silence was the law. Quaker girls and boys have the giggle in them, and after being pent up, it is very apt to break out into "an amusement." The author of the last sentence knows her subject; no contradiction is in order. So that the youth's table, as soon as the quiet abated, was, "within bounds," lively.

Dinner over, a few additional guests arrived. At candle-light, the tables were again laid. Best of Hyson tea, delicious biscuits, plum-cake and "hearts and rounds" (a Nantucket institution) were served. Tea over, yet a few more persons appeared for the evening; these were generally the "must-be-noticed" class. Having been put through this ordeal many times, as giver and receiver, each one understood the honor, but no one remained at home through ill-nature. Before the clock finished striking eight, there was handed round a large waiter holding at least forty-eight wine-glasses, each glass just two-thirds full of "home-made currant-juice." The young men and women of the family were taught to say, "Not any for me, I'm 'bliged to thee." That fashion of passing wine, *Authority* is happy to remark, has long since had the go-by; and, if anything as the evening beverage is desired at a Friends' wedding better than cold water, a little raspberry syrup supplies the deficiency.

At nine o'clock precisely, the guests, all three varieties, departed. The wedding was over.

LADY GODIVA.

HAVE you ever heard of Coventry, an old town not very far from London, where some of the streets are so narrow that no wagons can pass through them, and where the second stories of the quaint old mansions jut over so far into the streets that they almost touch each other?

It was a lovely morning in September. We had come from busy London, that immense city where one million people every year ride in the many railroads that are made under the houses, saying nothing of the millions who throng the streets above ground.

All the people know Americans at sight, and they looked at us as carefully as we at them. First we went to a tall church that Sir Christopher Wren, the

10

great architect, said was a masterpiece. Its tower and spire alone are three hundred and three feet high : that is about three times as high as the State House in Boston. The church was built nearly four hundred years before Columbus discovered America, and was given by a great earl to the monks — it is Protestant now — for " the repose of his soul." I suppose that means that he might get safely to Heaven.

But the thing which most interested us about Coventry was that here once lived a sweet and beautiful lady about whom the people never tire of telling you.

She was the wife of an earl who governed Coventry. He was immensely rich, but he taxed his subjects so that petitions came in every day to have them lowered. Finally, as all their beseeching did no good, the poor people came to his wife, Lady Godiva, to beg her to intercede for them. Her heart was touched, and she went to her husband, but he was angry, and bade her never to speak of it again.

Several months went by. He had been away to some wars in the northern part of England, and coming home, was so delighted to meet his wife and darling little boy, that he clasped them both to his heart, asking her if she needed anything to complete her happiness. She had money, an elegant home, and lived like a queen, but she could not be happy. She said, "While our people groan under oppression, the most luxurious entertainment can afford me no real enjoyment."

Leofric, her husband, again became violently angry, but said, since he had promised to do what she wished, he would keep his word; but she must ride on horseback, at noonday, from one end of the city to the other, with no clothing upon her. He supposed of course that she would never consent to this. For a moment, her noble womanly heart sank within her, and then she said, "I will go."

Seeing that her mind was made up, he ordered all the people to darken the fronts of their houses, and retire to the back parts of them, while the devoted lady took her lonely ride. When the appointed day came, the whole city was as still as death. Lady Godiva's beautiful white horse was brought to the palace. With a face as blanched as her charger, drawing her long dark hair like a scarf about her body, she mounted, and rode in solemn silence through all the principal streets. No sound was heard save that of the horse's hoofs, as the grateful people waited for their burdens to be lifted.

And when the ride was over, and the people opened their doors and unbarred their windows, a great cry of rejoicing went up from thousands, for Coventry was free. Lady Godiva, after founding several churches, died about the year 1059.

Every three or four years in Coventry a quaint procession still takes place in honor of this noble act of devotion to her people. The City Guard and High Constable lead the column. Then follows a beautiful woman clothed in a white linen dress, fitted close to her body, with long hair floating about her, and a large bunch of flowers in her hand, riding on a cream-colored horse. On either side of her are two city officials, dressed in green and scarlet. Two men come next bearing the sword and mace, emblems of the high authority of the mayor, followed by the mayor himself in his scarlet robes, trimmed with fur, wearing a cocked hat, and carrying a white wand in his hand. Then come the Sheriffs in their black

gowns; all the different trades of the city; the Odd
Fellows, Foresters, and other benevolent societies.

The principal characters of the show are attended
by beautiful children in costly habits, riding on
horseback. These children are so small that they
are obliged to sit in basket-work seats, which are
fastened to the horses' backs. The men who lead the
horses, walk without their coats, and are decorated
with a profusion of ribbons.

MOOLEY.

SOMEWHAT more than a hundred years ago, good Farmer Whitney, who lived in the little town of Spencer, in Massachusetts, found a new calf in his barn one April morning. The farmer looked at it, declared it a "likely heifer," and went in to tell the good news to his family. They all went to the barn at once—little Cyrus and Ben and John, and Dame Whitney with baby Lem in her arms.

Little Mooley stood by her mother quite bewildered at the number of her lively visitors. They admired her clear bright eyes, her brown dewy nose, shining coat and waxen hoofs; they patted her head, felt for her horns, and were delighted with the little white star in her forehead. She was pronounced "a very good calf." People in those days did not call everything which pleased them *splendid*, or *superb*, or

magnificent, as modern talkers do; these subjects of King George simply said Mooley was "a good calf"
— and so she was.

In a few days Mooley was taught to drink; Dame Whitney herself gave her her first lessons, after which she was left to the care of Cyrus, who was a "master hand with cattle," his father said. Cyrus brought in armfuls of the sweetest hay, and steeped it in water, to which he added a little meal and milk; for the poor calf had to share her mother's milk with the four little Whitneys. They with the neighbors' children played and romped with her sometimes, pulled her the tenderest grass, led her to water, taught her odd tricks; and one day when Cyrus and his father were out in the pasture they all heard the loud booming of the guns of Bunker Hill.

When Mooley was a well-grown heifer Mr. Whitney sold his farm and went to Talland, Connecticut. All their goods were packed upon an ox-cart, where the mother and baby, and sometimes one of the younger children, rode. The others, with the father and the live stock, Mooley among the rest, took up their line of march, on foot, toward their new home.

Once there, Mooley was left more than ever in Cyrus' care; for Mr. and Mrs. W. were engaged in making saltpetre, by leaching the earth dug from under old buildings, for the supply of gunpowder for the Federal army.

At last, one morning when Cyrus came down the ladder from the loft where he slept, he found his father preparing to go to war, while his mother stood before the fire which blazed in the wide chimney, turning her "nut-cakes" in the hissing fat, and proudly brushing away her tears.

Breakfast over, the good wife gave her "minute-man" a last drink of Mooley's milk, filled his knapsack with her cakes, and turned to her saltpetre works with more zeal than ever; for she was a resolute, fiery-hearted woman who loved her family and hated the king with equal fervor.

Even those who can remember the last war can have little idea of what our ancestors suffered during those sad seven years. Cyrus and his mother weeded the garden, fed the poultry, milked the cows — did their best. One day a hoop came off from the milk-pail — a milk-pail in those days was a clumsy affair with wooden hoops, looking more like a mackerel kit than a modern milk-pail. Mr. Whitney could easily have put on another hoop if he had been at home; but there was no one to do it now, as the cooper also had gone to war. So Mrs. W. sadly set the pail away and took the cream-pot, a wide-mouthed brown earthen jar, to the barn to milk in. She strained her milk into thick, heavy pans, earthen like the cream-pot, and skimmed it with a clam-shell. One night, I am sorry to say, Mooley kicked the cream-pot over, and while it went rolling across the barnyard she scampered away.

Poor Mrs. Whitney sat still on her milking-stool and cried! The children gathered round her: "It is not broken," they said consolingly. "Only a little milk is spilled!" "'Taint broke!" "'Taint broke, marm!"

"But it might have been," sobbed the poor, tired, troubled woman, as she prepared to pursue Mooley. To replace the pot would indeed have been a hard matter.

Mr. Whitney returned in a few months, and as it was becoming hard to get the earth for making salt-

petre, and as many of his neighbors were going to
Vermont, he set off on foot to see the new State. He
was not gone long, for it is said he walked eighty
miles some days between the rising and setting of the
sun.

He was much pleased with the new country, and
the family again prepared to move. I think, children,
you could hardly keep from laughing, spite of your
efforts to be polite, if you saw such a caravan coming.

In front of the ox-load of furniture was a seat
where some of them rode, and behind was strapped a
coop with some fowls in it. Mrs. Whitney rode on
horseback with a child behind her, and a baby in her
arms. Then there were two colts which Cyrus led
most of the way, and a few sheep, and Mooley and
her calves, which Ben and John helped to drive.
The entire family were dressed in warm woollen garments which Dame Whitney had made; carded, spun,
and woven the cloth from the wool shorn from their
own sheep, and then cut the garments, and made them
with thread of her spinning. Cyrus and his father
wore in addition short buckskin breeches buckled at
the knee.

Securely hidden in the midst of the load was one
of Mr. Whitney's long blue woollen stockings, knit to
come above the knee, tied up full of Spanish dollars.
" Not much march money," I hear some banker's boy
say; but it was more than most of the settlers carried
with them, and quite sufficient to make them a well-
to-do family in the new town where they were going.

Mrs. Whitney also carried with great care the
seeds of catnip and burdock and mullein and other
weeds which are now the pest of the Vermont farm-
ers. Indeed, many of the weeds we now despise
were in those days highly prized as medicines; and
every house-mother who went into the new country
carried with her not only bags of dried herbs, but
parcels of seeds to make sure the next year's supply.
Few doctors had yet gone to the new settlement, and
people were too poor to employ them except in
severest cases of sickness.

Thus these people took their way over rough
roads and through unbridged streams, more than a
hundred miles, in the bleak weather of December,
1780, just one hundred years ago ! I suppose they
got very cold and tired ; but they stopped at night at

the little country taverns, cared for their animals as best they could, ate their own luncheon, and drank a little milk which Mooley gave.

They found a pleasant home in Vermont. A new house was built, and a barn for Mooley and her calves — some of them grown to cows and oxen. Doubtless Mooley now thought she was settled for life; but, the war over, the settlers again became restless, and one morning Mr. Whitney came in to say that Mr. Dee wanted to buy Mooley.

"Buy Mooley?" they all exclaimed indignantly.

They were told that Mr. Dee was going to Cape Breton Island with his family, and they wanted Mooley for the milk supply and because she was known to be a good traveller.

So, although the children cried and Madam Whitney's stiff-starched cap-border fairly crackled with indignation, Mooley was sold; and they saw her trudge off toward the isle of Cape Breton — look on your maps and see where that is.

The Whitney children thereafter got a scanty supply of milk from a sheep, whose lamb they fed with bread and potatoes. This partly consoled them, and

Madam Whitney was very glad to have a little money to help the new church of which Mr. Whitney had just been made deacon; but still they all often thought and longed to hear of Mooley.

Postal communication was almost impossible in those days; postage was very high, and post-offices rare in the thinly settled parts of the country. Cards were unheard of, letters seldom written. When letters were written they were carried to the tavern and thrust behind strips of basket-stuff tacked to the wall in the bar-room; and travellers were accustomed to look over these letters and carry along those which were to go on their route, as far as possible, and leave them at the nearest tavern, when some other traveller would take them. Think of that, children, who send letters to your friends in California in less than a week!

In this way, or some other, Mrs. Whitney heard, a year after Mooley went away, that she arrived safe in Cape Breton Island, and was again a loyal subject of King George III.

THE GIRL THAT HAD PA-
TIENCE TO PRACTISE.

I HATE him! Yes, I do! and I never will take another lesson! See if I do!" This was said with emphasis.

Mrs. Gordon looked out of the parlor window to find that the speaker was her own little daughter. Madge was a bright, active girl with lovely chestnut hair, blue eyes and red cheeks. A pet at home and a favorite at school, it was not strange that she was imperious; she enjoyed music, but she "hated practice."

Mrs. Gordon looked thoughtful. She desired Madge to become an accurate musician, and she felt that Professor Dartrum was a judicious teacher. A moment later the parlor door was pushed open and

Madge stood there. There was a look of defiance in her deep blue eyes.

" Let us hear all about it," said Mrs. Gordon, making a place for Madge and her two young friends on the sofa. Then followed a brief narration of the very strict rules, and the torture to which she was every day subject.

" Miss Craven is not half as strict — say I may take of Miss Craven, mamma ! " Madge concluded.

For answer Mrs. Gordon said very gently, " Before we decide let me narrate something that I have read of a young girl whose teacher was far more exacting than Professor Dartrum."

" That could never be ! " exclaimed Madge.

" Will you have the story ? "

" Yes, yes ! " cried three voices in chorus.

" As I shall leave you to guess the name of the young girl, you will need to pay particular attention," continued Mrs. Gordon. " The sleepy old place in which our heroine lived, possibly had something to do in fostering the love of music in her breast until it burst into a flame bright enough to illumine two continents."

Here Madge felt that she had guessed the name.

"This sleepy old town," continued Mrs. Gordon, "had a theatre where the little girl was accustomed to go with her father. He was flute-player in the theatre, and organist in the famous old cathedral. At last, from following the musicians so closely, she longed to play herself. The flute did not suit her small mouth; but the violin—yes, she would have a violin !

"'A violin ! nothing could be more absurd,' her relatives declared; and aunt Caroline insisted that her father must not indulge the child in this way—only boys played violins. However, this little girl kept on asking, and at last her father brought home the smallest violin that he could possibly buy. And now for lessons ! M. Simon, the teacher, lived a good distance away. It did not matter : three times a week she took the long walk through the Rue Voltaire across the crowded Place where the theatre stood, past the handsome stores and over the bridge, and then along a narrow street till the gray towers of the old chateau came in sight.

"First she must learn to stand—now to rest on her left foot with the right partly in front; then how to hold her violin—how it should rest on her shoulder and how to grasp and support it. Hold it perfectly still for ten minutes! Then lay it down for a few minutes' rest! Take it up again and hold it firm!

" Patiently now she bent her small fingers over the strings, as if to touch a chord — head erect, left arm bent and brought forward so that she could see her elbow under the violin. Then she must stand perfectly still with the right arm hanging down naturally. No bow, of course. She must first learn to sustain the weight of the violin and accustom her arm to its shape. In silence, and motionless, she held the instrument.

" For two or three weeks she did this and nothing more.

" Then the bow was placed in her right hand. Now rest it lightly on the strings and draw it down slowly and steadily. Not a sound! No, there was no rosin on the bow, and it slipped over the strings in silence.

" Two hours every day, nothing but positions and dumb motions: not even finger exercises. Simply to learn to stand, to put the fingers in the right place, and to make the right motions with the bow. Very often her poor arms would ache, and her legs become

11

stiff with standing. Then her teacher had a temper, and was at times fearfully cross. Tears stood in her eyes; but no word of complaint ever was uttered. She was going to play, and this was the way to learn.

"At home the same thing was repeated. Three hours' practice every day with the dumb violin — and this for three full months.

"Now she has rosin on her bow. The exercises are all written out with a pen by her master. Long-sustained notes by the hour. The bow hardly moved, so slowly did she draw it up and down. If she obtained nothing else, she would have a strong, clear tone, and learn to make a grand, full sweep with her bow. Slowly and patiently she crept along, sometimes in the morning, sometimes late at night, listening to instructions and playing over the exercises.

"Seven hours every day! Scales in every key; running passages of every imaginable character — nearly a year of dry scales.

"One day a famous musical director put up at the Hotel de France. Would he listen to her playing? Yes.

"She sat in her usual place in the orchestra all the

evening, and then, near midnight, with her violin under her arm, called at the Hotel de France. The great artist had been treated to a banquet, and was still sitting in the dining-room. There were goblets and champagne glasses on the table, and after talking about music for a few moments, he took a fork, and gently tapping on a wine-glass, asked what note it was. It was E. And this one? A. And this one? D. And so on. He was greatly pleased with the experiment, and said he would hear her play. 'Only, you must mind, I don't like false notes.'

"' I never give 'em, sir.'

" He laughed, and she began to play. She was a bold, sturdy player, and astonished the director with the graceful sweep of her small arm. At the close he complimented her in a cordial manner, and hoped she would go on with her studies. 'Oh ! she would ; she meant to study all the time.'

"The first real piece was a grand occasion. She played it through hundreds of times. Hours were spent over one note. A week on a single page. One passage she could not get right : forty-seven times she played it before her master would let her off.

No matter, she must play it right if it took all day. Tears dropped on the violin, the master was still more enraged. At last she did it right, played it over several times, went home, and never played it wrong again in her life.

"At last there was to be a grand concert — something quite out of the common course; and it was decided to bring out this young musician with her wonderful violin-playing. The Italian opera, the French opera, the dramatic corps, all the grand families, every musician in that old city, bought a ticket.

"The concert began and went on. The orchestra played, and the artists sang, and then there was a little rustle and hush of expectation as they brought in a box for the child to stand upon so that all could see her.

"And then a slight, blue-eyed girl, in a white dress, white satin shoes, and a pink sash, appeared.

"At the piano sat her teacher; and her father stood by her side to turn the leaves of her music.

"But a moment before she had been carried away with the pink sash and dainty satin shoes; now she put the violin to her shoulder, and stood ready to play.

"The tone came, strong, full and true. The notes were in exact time. The people were hushed to a painful silence. In his excitement her father turned two leaves — the small player inclined her head and in a pretty, lisping whisper said:

"'You've turned two pages, papa.' The page was turned back without a pause, and the music went on. It was a brilliant rendering of a most difficult composition.

"It seemed as if the great musicians, the painters and the people *en masse* never would stop clapping and cheering. The leader of the orchestra offered, in the name of all the musicians, to crown her young head with a wreath of roses. The attempt was amusing — the wreath slipped over her shoulders, and fell to the floor, and there she stood in the midst of it!

"Then they brought a wonderful Paris doll, and set her quite wild with joy by presenting it to her.

"With the doll under one arm and the violin under the other, she bowed her thanks from the middle of the wreath.

"Then they cheered again and laughed and stormed her with flowers."

Mrs. Gordon paused.   Madge and her associates were on their feet.

"I am glad you told us — we cannot guess — only, mamma, a great genius would not have had to do all this," said Madge.

"Only genius would have been patient — in other words, patience and constant drill give genius wings," answered Mrs. Gordon.

"Tell us, please, and we will practise like her, without any more words," came frankly.

"*Camilla Urso*," answered Mrs. Gordon.